616

LIFELINES

"Children of The New Ballet School," *by Jim Varriale*

LIFELINES

A Poetry Anthology Patterned
on the Stages of Life

Selected and introduced by

LEONARD S. MARCUS

Dutton Children's Books   New York

for Jacob Henry Marcus

Library of Congress Cataloging-in-Publication Data

Lifelines / selected by Leonard S. Marcus.

p.   cm.

Summary: A collection of poems by such authors as William Blake,
Elizabeth Bishop, and Thomas Hardy.

ISBN 0-525-45164-1

1. Young adult poetry, American.   2. Young adult poetry, English.
[1. American poetry—Collections.   2. English poetry—Collections.]
I. Marcus, Leonard S.

PS586.3.L54 1994   821.008'0352054—dc20   93-26413   CIP AC

Published in the United States 1994 by Dutton Children's Books,
a division of Penguin Books USA Inc.
375 Hudson Street, New York, New York 10014

Designed by Amy Berniker
Printed in U.S.A.
First Edition
3 5 7 9 10 8 6 4 2

CONTENTS

Three ▪ ON SUCH A HILL

INTRODUCTION

The human life cycle has been compared to the four seasons and the twelve months of the year; to the course from dawn to dark of a single day; to a journey along a road or a river; to a climb up a flight of stairs to maturity, followed by a descent down a companion flight to old age and death. Each of these vivid analogies is centuries old. It seems that people have always needed metaphorical maps to help them picture—and come to terms with—the main outlines of their own, and everyone's, life story.

All the traditional life-cycle metaphors were the invention of poets or of people thinking poetically. Shakespeare plainly relished the challenge of adding to the stock of fresh depictions of this most human of themes. In his comedy *As You Like It,* for instance, the great playwright offers up the beguiling suggestion that life itself is a play, with infancy the first act, childhood the second, and so on until—alas!— we take our final bow.

Other poets have focused on particular stages or moments of the cycle, exploring up close the hopes, longings, and insights typical, for example, of the very young or of the not-quite-middle-aged. In this book, you will find a wide range of poems of this "up close" variety. The poems do not tell a single, continuous, or even altogether consistent story. They do not define borders as cleanly and clearly as a map does. My hope, though, is that the poems in this collection will provide you with a good many starting points for viewing your own, and other people's, life experiences from an enriched perspective.

The majority of the poems come from the United States, but I have also chosen work by poets from England, Ireland, Russia, Romania, China, India, Burma, Israel, and Persia (the old name for Iran). Many are twentieth century; one dates from as early as the eighth century. The poems from other cultures and historical periods are offered in part as invitations to ask: Granted everyone is born and dies, how much of what occurs in between is shaded, even shaped, by the beliefs, customs, and conditions specific to a certain society, locale, or era?

No doubt, plenty is given to us by our circumstances. It is also true, however, that poets are pathfinders whose imaginative inner journeys sometimes take them to the very edge of the common knowledge and wisdom of their culture and age.

Whenever that happens, the result is likely to be a poem that may be read and remembered everywhere. In compiling *Lifelines,* I have searched for accessible, funny, moving, passionate, memorable poems that I felt might belong in this rare and mysterious company of universal poetry.

The poems are arranged in four sections: infancy and childhood; adolescence and young adulthood; the prime of life and middle age; old age and death. I chose this plan not because I wished to align the book with the familiar seasonal metaphor for the life cycle, but because a four-part division seemed a flexible framework in which to present poems with diverse, even conflicting, views of the nature of growing up, coming of age, accepting responsibility, facing mortality. There are, of course, no guarantees that every one of us will actually live out the complete cycle, whatever the outlines we imagine for it. That stark reality is also acknowledged in these pages.

"Fear is what quickens me," said James Wright, one of the poets whose work follows. The best poets write as if their lives depend on it. To understand this, imagine yourself in a pitch-dark room. You start to wonder if you are all alone there. You wonder if you are not in some danger. Your thoughts and emotions race ahead to fill the void.

In a similar manner, a poet becomes immersed in an image or memory or intuition, or in one of life's perennial questions—What is love like? Why must we die? Why must *I* die?—and with words for lanterns tries to write his or her way out of the pitch-dark state of not-knowing.

As readers we have the luxury of breathing a bit easier, of having our way lit by the words of others. I hope that you will find much to enjoy in *Lifelines.* And I hope that you will let yourself be touched by the urgency and ardor with which the poets of this collection have set about the mysterious work of examining their own life stories for traces of yours and mine.

LIFELINES

"Playhouse, 1987," *by Abelardo Morell*

1

SMALL TRAVELLER

from To a New-Born Child

Small traveller from an unseen shore,
By mortal eye ne'er seen before,
    To you, good morrow.

William Cosmo Monkhouse

Infant Joy

"I have no name:
I am but two days old."
What shall I call thee?
"I happy am,
Joy is my name."
Sweet joy befall thee!

Pretty joy!
Sweet joy but two days old,
Sweet joy I call thee:
Thou dost smile,
I sing the while,
Sweet joy befall thee!

William Blake

To Miss Charlotte Pulteney
in Her Mother's Arms

Timely blossom, infant fair,
Fondling of a happy pair,
Every morn and every night,
Their solicitous delight,
Sleeping, waking, still at ease,
Pleasing, without skill to please,
Little gossip, blithe and hale,
Tattling many a broken tale,
Singing many a tuneless song,
Lavish of a heedless tongue,
Simple maiden, void of art,
Babbling out the very heart,
Yet abandoned to thy will,
Yet imagining no ill,
Yet too innocent to blush,
Like the linlet in the bush,
To the mother-linnet's note
Moduling her slender throat,
Chirping forth thy petty joys,
Wanton in the change of toys,
Like the linnet green in May,
Flitting to each bloomy spray,
Wearied then, and glad of rest,
Like the linlet in the nest.
This thy present happy lot,
This, in time, will be forgot:

Other pleasures, other cares,
Ever-busy time prepares;
And thou shalt in thy daughter see
This picture, once, resembled thee.

Ambrose Philips

Conch

Hold a baby to your ear
   As you would a shell:
Sounds of centuries you hear
   New centuries foretell.

Who can break a baby's code?
   And which is the older—
The listener or his small load?
   The held or the holder?

E. B. White

To David — At Six Months

Sometimes, my little son, I have become,
Under your long, cool stare, uncertain of our ages—
And this is not a reasonable power in one so newly born.
In moments like these
Fond foolishness dies upon my lips
And silly names made for a child
Become unfit for one whose manner is detached, contained;
Whose quiet gaze seems leveled at my heart
As though in search of something you cannot explain.

Born of my body, yet not thus by me possessed,
I must remind myself,
Having now a sense of time, of briefness, and the farthest
                                                    stars:
Of how we meet to touch and speak and love each other
For the smallest space—
Then go our separate ways again.

But now, because your mood has changed
And you consent to see me and to laugh like any babe,
Enchanting, sly, and full of some mysterious,
Sudden joy,
I lean to catch the fragrance of your flesh.

To hold you close—and in this pause
To store within my heart for later days
Your wondering, upward look,
Your old, old air of grave surprise.

Eleanor Cameron

"This is my name"

This is my name
I have my own name

I look in the mirror
And I'm still the same

I hide in the hall
But I'm not lost at all

Just like a bell
That hangs on a cat

Wherever I go
It can bring me back

   (Call Patty, Patty, Patty)

Norman Rosten

Mutterings Over the Crib of a Deaf Child

"How will he hear the bell at school
Arrange the broken afternoon,
And know to run across the cool
Grasses where the starlings cry,
Or understand the day is gone?"

Well, someone lifting cautious brows
Will take the measure of the clock.
And he will see the birchen boughs
Outside the sagging dark from the sky,
And the shade crawling upon the rock.

"And how will he know to rise at morning?
His mother has other sons to waken,
She has the stove she must build to burning
Before the coals of the night-time die,
And he never stirs when he is shaken."

I take it the air affects the skin,
And you remember, when you were young,
Sometimes you could feel the dawn begin,
And the fire would call you, by and by,
Out of the bed and bring you along.

"Well, good enough. To serve his needs
All kinds of arrangements can be made.
But what will you do if his finger bleeds?
Or a bobwhite whistles invisibly
And flutes like an angel off in the shade?"

He will learn pain. And, as for the bird,
It is always darkening when that comes out.
I will putter as though I had not heard,
And lift him into my arms and sing
Whether he hears my song or not.

James Wright

"Baby, baby"

Baby, baby,
Stick your head
In gravy!

Anonymous

When I Was Three

When I was three I had a friend
Who asked me why bananas bend,
I told him why, but now I'm four
I'm not so sure. . . .

Richard Edwards

Human Affection

Mother, I love you so.
Said the child, I love you more than I know.
She laid her head on her mother's arm,
And the love between them kept them warm.

Stevie Smith

The Hired Man's Faith in Children

I believe *all* childern's good,
Ef they're only *understood*,—
Even *bad* ones 'pears to me
'S jes' as good as they kin be!

James Whitcomb Riley

"God made the bees"

God made the bees,
   The bees make honey;
We do the work,
   The teacher gets the money.

Anonymous

The Swing

How do you like to go up in a swing,
   Up in the air so blue?
Oh, I do think it the pleasantest thing
   Ever a child can do!

Up in the air and over the wall,
   Till I can see so wide,
Rivers and trees and cattle and all
   Over the countryside—

Till I look down on the garden green
   Down on the roof so brown—
Up in the air I go flying again,
   Up in the air and down!

Robert Louis Stevenson

First Song

Then it was dusk in Illinois, the small boy
After an afternoon of carting dung
Hung on the rail fence, a sapped thing
Weary to crying. Dark was growing tall
And he began to hear the pond frogs all
Calling on his ear with what seemed their joy.

Soon their sound was pleasant for a boy
Listening in the smoky dusk and the nightfall
Of Illinois, and from the fields two small
Boys came bearing cornstalk violins
And they rubbed the cornstalk bows with resins
And the three sat there scraping of their joy.

It was now fine music the frogs and the boys
Did in the towering Illinois twilight make
And into dark in spite of a shoulder's ache
A boy's hunched body loved out of a stalk
The first song of his happiness, and the song woke
His heart to the darkness and into the sadness of joy.

Galway Kinnell

In the Waiting Room

In Worcester, Massachusetts,
I went with Aunt Consuelo
to keep her dentist's appointment
and sat and waited for her
in the dentist's waiting room.
It was winter. It got dark
early. The waiting room
was full of grown-up people,
arctics and overcoats,
lamps and magazines.
My aunt was inside
what seemed like a long time
and while I waited I read
the *National Geographic*
(I could read) and carefully
studied the photographs:
the inside of a volcano,
black, and full of ashes;
then it was spilling over
in rivulets of fire.
Osa and Martin Johnson
dressed in riding breeches,
laced boots, and pith helmets.
A dead man slung on a pole
—"Long Pig," the caption said.
Babies with pointed heads
wound round and round with string;
black, naked women with necks

wound round and round with wire
like the necks of light bulbs.
Their breasts were horrifying.
I read it right straight through.
I was too shy to stop.
And then I looked at the cover:
the yellow margins, the date.

Suddenly, from inside,
came an *oh!* of pain
—Aunt Consuelo's voice—
not very loud or long.
I wasn't at all surprised;
even then I knew she was
a foolish, timid woman.
I might have been embarrassed,
but wasn't. What took me
completely by surprise
was that it was *me:*
my voice, in my mouth.
Without thinking at all
I was my foolish aunt,
I—we—were falling, falling,
our eyes glued to the cover
of the *National Geographic,*
February, 1918.

I said to myself: three days
and you'll be seven years old.
I was saying it to stop

the sensation of falling off
the round, turning world
into cold, blue-black space.
But I felt: you are an *I*,
you are an *Elizabeth,*
you are one of *them.*
Why should you be one, too?
I scarcely dared to look
to see what it was I was.
I gave a sidelong glance
—I couldn't look any higher—
at shadowy gray knees,
trousers and skirts and boots
and different pairs of hands
lying under the lamps.
I knew that nothing stranger
had ever happened, that nothing
stranger could ever happen.
Why should I be my aunt,
or me, or anyone?
What similarities—
boots, hands, the family voice
I felt in my throat, or even
the *National Geographic*
and those awful hanging breasts—
held us all together
or made us all just one?
How—I didn't know any
word for it—how "unlikely" . . .
How had I come to be here,

like them, and overhear
a cry of pain that could have
got loud and worse but hadn't?

The waiting room was bright
and too hot. It was sliding
beneath a big black wave,
another, and another.

Then I was back in it.
The War was on. Outside,
in Worcester, Massachusetts,
were night and slush and cold,
and it was still the fifth
of February, 1918.

Elizabeth Bishop

Ethiopia
for Tifa

Seven years without milk
means everyone dances for joy
on your birthday
but when you clap   your hands
break at the wrist
and even grandmother's ghee
cannot mend
the delicate embroideries
of bone.

Audre Lorde

Spring and Fall:

to a young child

Márgarét, áre you gríeving
Over Goldengrove unleaving?
Leáves líke the things of man, you
With your fresh thoughts care for, can you?
Áh! ás the heart grows older
It will come to such sights colder
By and by, nor spare a sigh
Though worlds of wanwood leafmeal lie;
And yet you wíll weep and know why.
Now no matter, child, the name:
Sórrow's spríngs áre the same.
Nor mouth had, no nor mind, expressed
What heart heard of, ghost guessed:
It ís the blight man was born for,
It is Margaret you mourn for.

Gerard Manley Hopkins

A Poem by Garnie Braxton

"Garnie, I wish I was a sea gull."

"Yeah, me too.
  And when you want to get warm
  All you got to do
  Is put on your feathers
  And fly away to the south.

  I been there once."

James Wright

"1966, East 100th Street," *by Bruce Davidson*

2

I AM OLD ENOUGH

José Cruz

 75 lbs.—Get serious.
100 lbs.—A little better.
125 lbs.—Now you're talkin'.
150 lbs.—I can do it.
Whenever I feel the weight of the world
On my shoulders, I go to the gym and work out.
It makes me feel good about myself.
When I crouch to snatch the bar,
I don't think about nothin' else
'Cept puttin' it over my head.
I don't think about
School,
My life,
My future,
Nothin'.
Put on more weights.
I can handle it, man.
No sweat.

Mel Glenn

Dresses

Twelve and ugly
always wearing hand-me-downs
(O beautiful dresses I cannot have you)
and Mrs. Brown
"went to town, with her panties hanging down,"
deaconess of my father's church in Tulsa.
Bringing boxes of old clothes,
she called them presents for me,
muddy bumpy ladies dresses,
the kind you pin brooches on
between the bosoms (or breasts
as it said in *Song of Solomon* that summer).
Mrs. Brown being Christian,
inviting me to milk her cows
in the country. Three days in the country.
Mrs. Brown saying "it is hot dear,
wouldn't you like to take off all your clothes
while the men are away?"
Afraid to say no,
I wore my underwear and hated her
lying wrinkled and naked in the sun on her bed.

Hurt that I wanted to go home,
she never sent presents after that.
But other boxes came. Other people's clothes—
faded, too tight in the hips or saggy on top.
"It looks lovely dear," they would say, dreaming
of their kindnesses, how Christ would forgive them if

he came to earth and found them sitting
in the movie house on Sunday.
(O beautiful dresses I cannot have you)
Ribbons pink and blue satin
streaming from the hair of Ginger Stinson who let boys
kiss her and was popular.
Maroon velvet curtains in the gymnasium
hiding games behind them—*Phantom of the Opera.*

When I was a child I spoke as a child
I thought as a child I understood
as a child.
But how can one put away childish things?
Mrs. Brown's dresses still button to my chin.

Kathleen Fraser

The Brothers: Two Saltimbanques

Two boys stand at the end of the full train
Looking out the back, out the sides, turning
Toward each other. Their arms and shoulders brush
As the train shakes. They've been to the ballpark
Together, and can prove it with the huge
Red and blue scorecards in their hands. A sense
Of repeating in the shapes of the ears,
In the bearing of the clefted, young chins.
The older brother is perhaps fifteen,
The other, twelve? A gold of Indians
In summer faces, the color of their
Like hair, which is cut short, though with more bronze
In the younger. The brows of the older
Are surprisingly rich. And this young man
Is ripe with strength, his long face keen shaped,
Arrogant, rather sad about the eyes,
The face not yet tight. They wear green t-shirts
(Perhaps for some school sports?), their khaki pants
Sagging from the day in the sun. The two
Brothers slowly sway together with the
Motion of the train. The younger works hard
At his great scorecard. Now the older son
Bends to whisper: mixed, uncontrolled higher
And lower laughter runs over the train's
Screams, and raises heads out of newspapers.
Suddenly we strike a curve. The small one
Loses balance, and the other moves to
Steady him, leg and thigh muscles tight a-

gainst the steel weight of cars. They straighten. They
Smile, and the older boy's hand rests awhile
At his brother's side. Now as the train slows
A school of jets wings at the left windows
Tracking flame from the late sun. The boys lean
To the glass and the small one grins, gestur-
ing toward the planes, his long young arm poised,
Giving the lie to awkwardness at twelve
Catching for a passing moment the grace
Of what he felt. Now they move to the front
And get off. I watch them walk the platform
At the station. On the invitation
Of a vendor they buy Coke. They won't look
At the pencilled dirty word, with its figure,
On the margin of a sign scorecard red.
They start home together for supper and bed.

John Logan

The Conventionalist

Fourteen-year-old, why must you giggle and dote,
Fourteen-year-old, why are you such a goat?
I'm fourteen years old, that is the reason,
I giggle and dote in season.

Stevie Smith

We Real Cool

The Pool Players.
Seven at the Golden Shovel.

We real cool. We
Left school. We

Lurk late. We
Strike straight. We

Sing sin. We
Thin gin. We

Jazz June. We
Die soon.

Gwendolyn Brooks

Uncertain Admission

The sky looks down on me in aimless blues
The sun glares at me with a questioning light
The mountains tower over me with uncertain shadows
The trees sway in the bewildered breeze
The deer dance in perplexed rhythms
The ants crawl around me in untrusting circles
The birds soar above me with doubtful dips and dives.
They all, in their own way, ask the question,
Who are you, who are you?
I have to admit to them, to myself,
I am an Indian.

Frances Bazil

Poem

Instant coffee with slightly sour cream
in it, and a phone call to the beyond
which doesn't seem to be coming any nearer.
"Ah daddy, I wanna stay drunk many days"
on the poetry of a new friend
my life held precariously in the seeing
hands of others, their and my impossibilities.
Is this love, now that the first love
has finally died, where there were no impossibilities?

Frank O'Hara

Now Is the Month of Maying

Now is the month of maying,
When merry lads are playing
Each with his bonny lass
Upon the greeny grass.

The Spring, clad all in gladness,
Doth laugh at Winter's sadness,
And to the bagpipe's sound
The nymphs tread out their ground.

Fie then! why sit we musing,
Youth's sweet delight refusing?
Say, dainty nymphs, and speak,
Shall we play barley-break?

Anonymous

Brown Penny

I whispered, "I am too young."
And then, "I am old enough";
Wherefore I threw a penny
To find out if I might love.
"Go and love, go and love, young man,
If the lady be young and fair."
Ah, penny, brown penny, brown penny,
I am looped in the loops of her hair.

O love is the crooked thing,
There is nobody wise enough
To find out all that is in it,
For he would be thinking of love
Till the stars had run away
And the shadows eaten the moon.
Ah, penny, brown penny, brown penny,
One cannot begin it too soon.

William Butler Yeats

The River Merchant's Wife:
A Letter

While my hair was still cut straight across my forehead
I played about the front gate, pulling flowers.
You came by on bamboo stilts, playing horse,
You walked about my seat, playing with blue plums.
And we went on living in the village of Chokan:
Two small people, without dislike or suspicion.

At fourteen I married My Lord you.
I never laughed, being bashful.
Lowering my head, I looked at the wall.
Called to, a thousand times, I never looked back.

At fifteen I stopped scowling,
I desired my dust to be mingled with yours
Forever and forever and forever.
Why should I climb the look out?

At sixteen you departed,
You went into far Ku-to-yen, by the river of swirling eddies,
And you have been gone five months.
The monkeys make sorrowful noise overhead.

You dragged your feet when you went out.
By the gate now, the moss is grown, the different mosses,
Too deep to clear them away!
The leaves fall early this autumn, in wind.
The paired butterflies are already yellow with August

Over the grass in the West garden;
They hurt me. I grow older.
If you are coming down through the narrows of the river Kiang,
Please let me know beforehand,
And I will come out to meet you
                              As far as Cho-fu-Sa.

Rihaku,
translation by Ezra Pound

Runaway Teen

Any cold night I am hiding. Some people
come along. They stop on the bridge
and I listen. Water gurgles
and sings, but voices are clear as moonlight.

"We'll keep it for all of us—
the others don't need to share."
"How about Connie?—she wanted to be here."
"Forget about her." And they walk on.

In freezing rain that night I choose
my place:—in the wilderness, the loyalty
of chance. In time's clumsy attempts
anything can happen, and faith is a relic today.

It's hard being a person.
We all know that.

William Stafford

Eighteen

Wet streets. It has rained drops big as silver coins,
gold in the sun.
My mind charges the world like a bull.
Today I am eighteen.

The good rain batters me with crazy thoughts.
Look. Drops are warm and slow
as when I was in a carriage, pinned tight
in diapers, drenched and unchanged for an hour.

Yes, it rained as tomorrow, in the past, always.
The heart scrapes through time, is one heart.
My temples beat stronger than temples of time.

Like a common bum I think of drinking life,
but I am burnt, even by the hot stream of its juices.
I am eighteen.

Maria Banus,
translation by Willis Barnstone and Matei Calinescu

Paths

Going out into the fields of learning,
We shake the dew from the grasses.
All is new.
The paths we make through the wet grasses shine
As if with light.

They go where we take them, where they go.
Slow wings unfold, scarcely any
Motion happens but our heavy seeking.

Ant labors, hopper leaps away; too early for the bee,
The spider's silk hypotheses unfold
Tenacious, tenable.

Josephine Miles

Elegy for Jane

My Student, Thrown by a Horse

I remember the neckcurls, limp and damp as tendrils;
And her quick look, a sidelong pickerel smile;
And how, once startled into talk, the light syllables leaped for her,
And she balanced in the delight of her thought,
A wren, happy, tail into the wind,
Her song trembling the twigs and small branches.
The shade sang with her;
The leaves, their whispers turned to kissing;
And the mold sang in the bleached valleys under the rose.

Oh, when she was sad, she cast herself down into such a pure depth,
Even a father could not find her:
Scraping her cheek against straw;
Stirring the clearest water.

My sparrow, you are not here,
Waiting like a fern, making a spiny shadow.
The sides of wet stones cannot console me,
Nor the moss, wound with the last light.

If only I could nudge you from this sleep,
My maimed darling, my skittery pigeon.
Over this damp grave I speak the words of my love:
I, with no rights in this matter,
Neither father nor lover.

Theodore Roethke

The College Colonel

He rides at their head;
    A crutch by his saddle just slants in view,
One slung arm is in splints, you see,
        Yet he guides his strong steed—how coldly
            too.

He brings his regiment home—
    Not as they filed two years before,
But a remnant half-tattered, and battered, and
        worn,
Like castaway sailors, who—stunned
        By the surf's loud roar,
    Their mates dragged back and seen no more—
Again and again breast the surge,
    And at last crawl, spent, to shore.

A still rigidity and pale—
    An Indian aloofness lones his brow;
He has lived a thousand years
Compressed in battle's pains and prayers,
        Marches and watches slow.

There are welcoming shouts, and flags;
    Old men off hat to the Boy,
Wreaths from gay balconies fall at his feet,
    But to *him*—there comes alloy.

It is not that a leg is lost,
    It is not that an arm is maimed,
It is not that the fever has racked—
    Self he has long disclaimed.

But all through the Seven Days' Fight,
    And deep in the Wilderness grim,
And in the field-hospital tent,
    And Petersburg crater, and dim
Lean brooding in Libby, there came—
    Ah heaven!—what *truth* to him.

Herman Melville

R.A.F. (Aged Eighteen)

Laughing through clouds, his milk-teeth still unshed,
Cities and men he smote from overhead.
His deaths delivered, he returned to play
Childlike, with childish things not put away.

Rudyard Kipling

"Oh, rare Harry Parry"

Oh, rare Harry Parry,
When will you marry?
When apples and pears are ripe.
I'll come to your wedding
Without any bidding,
And dance and sing all the night.

Anonymous

"Sally, Sally Waters, sprinkle in the pan"

Sally, Sally Waters, sprinkle in the pan,
Hie Sally, hie Sally, for a young man.
Choose for the best
Choose for the worst
Choose for the prettiest that you like best.

Anonymous

from A Short Song of Congratulation

Long-expected one and twenty
  Lingering year at last is flown,
Pomp and pleasure, pride and plenty,
  Great Sir John, are all your own.

Loosened from the minor's tether,
  Free to mortgage or to sell,
Wild as wind, and light as feather,
  Bid the slaves of thrift farewell.

Call the Bettys, Kates, and Jennys,
  Every name that laughs at care,
Lavish of your grandsire's guineas,
  Show the spirit of an heir.

Samuel Johnson

Letter to N. Y.

For Louise Crane

In your next letter I wish you'd say
where you are going and what you are doing;
how are the plays, and after the plays
what other pleasures you're pursuing:

taking cabs in the middle of the night,
driving as if to save your soul
where the road goes round and round the park
and the meter glares like a moral owl,

and the trees look so queer and green
standing alone in big black caves
and suddenly you're in a different place
where everything seems to happen in waves,

and most of the jokes you just can't catch,
like dirty words rubbed off a slate,
and the songs are loud but somehow dim
and it gets so terribly late,

and coming out of the brownstone house
to the gray sidewalk, the watered street,
one side of the buildings rises with the sun
like a glistening field of wheat.

—Wheat, not oats, dear. I'm afraid
if it's wheat it's none of your sowing,
nevertheless I'd like to know
what you are doing and where you are going.

Elizabeth Bishop

"The Brown Sisters, Watertown, MA," *by Nicholas Nixon*

3

ON SUCH A HILL

My Heart Leaps Up

My heart leaps up when I behold
     A rainbow in the sky:
So was it when my life began;
So is it now I am a man;
So be it when I shall grow old,
     Or let me die!
The Child is father of the Man;
And I could wish my days to be
Bound each to each by natural piety.

William Wordsworth

On a Female Rope-Dancer

Whilst in her prime and bloom of years,
    Fair Celia trips the rope,
Alternately she moves our fears,
    Alternately our hope.

But when she sinks, or rises higher,
    Or graceful does advance,
We know not which we most admire,
    The dancer, or the dance.

Anonymous

I See A Truck

I see a truck mowing down a parade,
people getting up after to follow,
dragging a leg. On a corner
a cop stands idly swinging his club,
the sidewalks jammed with mothers
and baby carriages. No one screams
or speaks. From the tail end
of the truck a priest and a rabbi intone
their prayers, a jazz band bringing up
the rear, surrounded by dancers and lovers.
A bell rings and a paymaster drives through,
his wagon filled with pay envelopes
he hands out, even to those lying dead
or fornicating on the ground.
It is a holiday called
"Working for a Living."

David Ignatow

I Know I'm Not Sufficiently Obscure

I know I'm not sufficiently obscure
to please the critics—nor devious enough.
Imagery escapes me.
I cannot find those mild and gracious words
to clothe the carnage.
Blood is blood and murder's murder.
What's a lavender word for lynch?
Come, you pale poets, wan, refined and dreamy:
here is a black woman working out her guts
in a white man's kitchen
for little money and no glory.
How should I tell that story?
There is a black boy, blacker still from death,
face down in the cold Korean mud.
Come on with your effervescent jive
explain to him why he ain't alive.
Reword our specific discontent
into some plaintive melody,
a little whine, a little whimper,
not too much—and no rebellion!
God, no! Rebellion's much too corny.
You deal with finer feelings,
very subtle—an autumn leaf
hanging from a tree—I see a body!

Ray Durem

The Bride

Oh to be a bride
Brilliant in my curls
Under the white canopy
Of a modest veil!

How my hands tremble,
Bound by my icy rings!
The glasses gather, brimming
With red compliments.

At last the world says yes;
It wishes me roses and sons.
My friends stand shyly at the door,
Carrying love gifts.

Chemises in cellophane,
Plates, flowers, lace . . .
They kiss my cheeks, they marvel
I'm to be a wife.

Soon my white gown
Is stained with wine like blood;
I feel both lucky and poor
As I sit, listening, at the table.

Terror and desire
Loom in the forward hours.
My mother, the darling, weeps—
Mama is like the weather.

. . . My rich, royal attire
I lay aside on the bed.
I find I am afraid
To look at you, to kiss you.

Loudly the chairs are set
Against the wall, eternity . . .
My love, what more can happen
To you and to me?

Bella Akhmadulina,
translation by Stephen Stepanchev

The Marriage

The wind comes from opposite poles,
traveling slowly.

She turns in the deep air.
He walks in the clouds.

She readies herself,
shakes out her hair,

makes up her eyes,
smiles.

The sun warms her teeth,
the tip of her tongue moistens them.

He brushes the dust from his suit
and straightens his tie.

He smokes.
Soon they will meet.

The wind carries them closer.
They wave.

Closer, closer.
They embrace.

She is making a bed.
He is pulling off his pants.

They marry
and have a child.

The wind carries them off
in different directions.

The wind is strong, he thinks
as he straightens his tie.

I like this wind, she says
as she puts on her dress.

The wind unfolds.
The wind is everything to them.

Mark Strand

The Way

My love's manners in bed
are not to be discussed by me,
as mine by her
I would not credit comment upon gracefully.

Yet I ride by the margin of that lake in
the wood, the castle,
and the excitement of strongholds;
and have a small boy's notion of doing good.

Oh well, I will say here,
knowing each man,
let you find a good wife too,
and love her as hard as you can.

Robert Creeley

The Woman with Child

How I am held within a tranquil shell,
As if I too were close within a womb,
I too enfolded as I fold the child.

As the tight bud enwraps the pleated leaf,
The blossom furled like an enfolded fan,
So life enfold me as I fold my flower.

As water lies within a lovely bowl,
I lie within my life, and life again
Lies folded fast within my living cell.

The apple waxes at the blossom's root,
And like the moon I mellow to the round
Full circle of my being, till I too

Am ripe with living and my fruit is grown.
Then break the shell of life. We shall be born,
My child and I, together, to the sun.

Freda Laughton

Show Me The Way

The rose-apple is in fruit
the waters rise
the toddy fruit falls
and slow rain comes down
incessantly.

I would like to go home
to my mother;
husband, show me the way.

Anonymous,
translation by U Win Pe

Turning Thirty

This spring, you'd swear it actually gets dark earlier.
At the elegant new restaurants downtown
your married friends lock glances over the walnut torte:
it's ten o'clock. They have important jobs
and go to bed before midnight. Only you
walking alone up the dazzling avenue
still feel a girl's excitement, for the thousandth time
you enter your life as though for the first time,
as an immigrant enters a huge, mysterious capital:
Paris, New York. So many wide plazas, so many marble addresses!
Home, you write feverishly
in all five notebooks at once, then faint into bed
dazed with ambition and too many cigarettes.

Well, what's wrong with that? Nothing, except
really you don't believe wrinkles mean character
and know it's an ominous note
that the Indian skirts flapping on the sidewalk racks
last summer looked so gay you wanted them all
but now are marked clearer than price tags: not for you.
Oh, what were you doing, why weren't you paying attention
that piercingly blue day, not a cloud in the sky,
when suddenly "choices"
ceased to mean "infinite possibilities"
and became instead "deciding what to do without"?
No wonder you're happiest now
riding on trains from one lover to the next.

In those black, night-mirrored windows
a wild white face, operatic, still enthralls you:
a romantic heroine,
suspended between lives, suspended between destinations.

Katha Pollitt

The Parent

Children aren't happy with nothing to ignore,
And that's what parents were created for.

Ogden Nash

Ave Maria

Mothers of America
                          let your kids go to the movies!
get them out of the house so they won't know what you're up to
it's true that fresh air is good for the body
                                          but what about the soul
that grows in darkness, embossed by silvery images
and when you grow old as grow old you must
                                          they won't hate you
they won't criticise you they won't know
                          they'll be in some glamorous country
they first saw on a Saturday afternoon or playing hookey

they may even be grateful to you
                          for their first sexual experience
which only cost you a quarter
                          and didn't upset the peaceful home
they will know where candy bars come from
                          and gratuitous bags of popcorn
as gratuitous as leaving the movie before it's over
with a pleasant stranger whose apartment is in the
                          Heaven on Earth Bldg
near the Williamsburg Bridge
                          oh mothers you will have made the little tykes
so happy because if nobody does pick them up in the movies
they won't know the difference
                          and if somebody does it'll be sheer gravy
and they'll have been truly entertained either way

instead of hanging around the yard
                              or up in their room
                                        hating you
prematurely since you won't have done anything horribly
                                        mean yet
except keeping them from the darker joys
                              it's unforgivable the latter
so don't blame me if you won't take this advice
                              and the family breaks up
and your children grow old and blind in front of a TV set
                                        seeing
movies you wouldn't let them see when they were young

Frank O'Hara

With Kit, Age 7, at the Beach

We would climb the highest dune,
from there to gaze and come down:
the ocean was performing;
we contributed our climb.

Waves leapfrogged and came
straight out of the storm.
What should our gaze mean?
Kit waited for me to decide.

Standing on such a hill,
what would you tell your child?
That was an absolute vista.
Those waves raced far, and cold.

"How far could you swim, Daddy,
in such a storm?"
"As far as was needed," I said,
and as I talked, I swam.

William Stafford

"My son, in whose face there is already a sign"

My son, in whose face there is already a sign
of eagle—
like a daring prefix to your life,
let me kiss you once more while you still love it,
softly, like this.
Before you become a hairy Esau of open fields
be for a little while
soft-skinned Jacob for my blind hands.

Your brain is well packed in your skull,
efficiently folded for life. Had it stayed
spread out you might have been happier,
a large sheet of happiness without memory.

I'm on my way from believing in God
and you're on your way toward it: This too
is a meeting point of a father and a son.

It's evening now. The earthball is cooling,
clouds that have never lain with a woman
pass overhead in the sky, the desert
starts breathing into our ears,
and all the generations
squeeze a bar mitzvah for you.

Yehuda Amichai

Unwanted

The poster with my picture on it
Is hanging on the bulletin board in the Post Office.

I stand by it hoping to be recognized
Posing first full face and then profile

But everybody passes by and I have to admit
The photograph was taken some years ago.

I was unwanted then and I'm unwanted now
Ah guess ah'll go up echo mountain and crah.

I wish someone would find my fingerprints somewhere
Maybe on a corpse and say, You're it.

Description: Male, or reasonably so
Complexion white, but not lily-white.

Thirty-fivish, and looks it lately
Five-feet-nine and one-hundred-thirty pounds: no physique

Black hair going gray, hairline receding fast
What used to be curly, now fuzzy

Brown eyes starey under beetling brow
Mole on chin, probably will become a wen

It is perfectly obvious that he was not popular at school
No good at baseball, and wet his bed.

His aliases tell his history: Dumbell, Good-for-nothing,
Jewboy, Fieldinsky, Skinny, Fierce Face, Greaseball, Sissy.

Warning: This man is not dangerous, answers to any name
Responds to love, don't call him or he will come.

Edward Field

Middle-Age Enthusiasms

To M. H.

We passed where flag and flower
Signalled a jocund throng;
We said: "Go to, the hour
Is apt!"—and joined the song;
And, kindling, laughed at life and care,
Although we knew no laugh lay there.

We walked where shy birds stood
Watching us, wonder-dumb;
Their friendship met our mood;
We cried: "We'll often come:
We'll come morn, noon, eve, everywhen!"
—We doubted we should come again.

We joyed to see strange sheens
Leap from quaint leaves in shade;
A secret light of greens
They'd for their pleasure made.
We said: "We'll set such sorts as these!"
—We knew with night the wish would cease.

"So sweet the place," we said,
"Its tacit tales so dear,
Our thoughts, when breath has sped,

Will meet and mingle here!" . . .
"Words!" mused we. "Passed the mortal door,
Our thoughts will reach this nook no more."

Thomas Hardy

The Fisherwoman

She took from her basket four fishes
and carved each into four slices
and scaled them with her long knife,
this fisherwoman, and wrapped them;
and took four more and worked
in this rhythm through the day,
each action ending on a package
of old newspapers; and when it came
to close, dark coming upon the streets,
she had done one thing, she felt, well,
making one complete day.

David Ignatow

Men at Forty

Men at forty
Learn to close softly
The doors to rooms they will not be
Coming back to.

At rest on a stair landing,
They feel it moving
Beneath them now like the deck of a ship,
Though the swell is gentle.

And deep in mirrors
They rediscover
The face of the boy as he practices tying
His father's tie there in secret

And the face of that father,
Still warm with the mystery of lather.
They are more fathers than sons themselves now.
Something is filling them, something

That is like the twilight sound
Of the crickets, immense,
Filling the woods at the foot of the slope
Behind their mortgaged houses.

Donald Justice

Embassy

As evening fell the day's oppression lifted;
Far peaks came into focus; it had rained:
Across wide lawns and cultured flowers drifted
The conversation of the highly trained.

Two gardeners watched them pass and priced their shoes:
A chauffeur waited, reading in the drive,
For them to finish their exchange of views;
It seemed a picture of the private life.

Far off, no matter what good they intended,
The armies waited for a verbal error
With all the instruments for causing pain:

And on the issue of their charm depended
A land laid waste, with all its young men slain,
Its women weeping, and its towns in terror.

W. H. Auden

Let No Charitable Hope

Now let no charitable hope
Confuse my mind with images
Of eagle and of antelope:
I am in nature none of these.

I was, being human, born alone;
I am, being woman, hard beset;
I live by squeezing from a stone
The little nourishment I get.

In masks outrageous and austere
The years go by in single file;
But none has merited my fear,
And none has quite escaped my smile.

Elinor Wylie

Beach Party Given by
T. Shaughnessy for the Sisters

Seven nuns went wading in the sea,
They wore no shoes,
They lined up along the shore and the shore washed out
And flooded back to the very knee.
A rough but good shore and sea.

The seaweed and the wimple habits were,
Close and alive,
Both cumbrous but of will designed and worn.
For every nun the sea was good to her,
And alike their habits were.

It was so rough a day, like cormorants more
You would have thought
The nuns would take to nest, but still they cried and stayed.
They were like to the devout sea, and to the shore
They sisters were.

Josephine Miles

One for the Road

On the old bicycle the plumber brought me
Saint Christopher gleams by the traffic bell.
"Good as new." He tapped a rusty fender.
"The girl who rode it moved to Florida.
She was some kind of teacher, too," he grinned.

No baskets, saddlebags, license, or lights.
Eight novels crammed into my backpack—
excessive as a life vest stuffed with stones—
I pedal two miles to the travel agent
to pay for my son's airline ticket home.

Twenty years ago I jogged to market
bearing the light burden of him, bobbing
against my back. Singing to rooks and jays,
he dipped his head under the sky's wing.
He was lighter than my dictionary.

On the threshold, when I set him down,
my muscles quivered, light flooded my bones.
I was a still lake holding up the sky.
Now in his empty room, I hang the map
that flopped out of the *National Geographic*.

Start with what you know, I tell my students.
Detroit, New York, Ann Arbor, Battle Creek—
the roads that spider off from towns I know
are red as arteries that serve the heart
and bring fresh news to all its distant cities,

Madison, Minneapolis–St. Paul.
At his first solo flight away from home
wearing the new jeans he'd bought for school,
his father gave him a gold medal. "Given
for good conduct all the years we had you,
and for good luck." A talisman, a blessing,
friendly as butter: Christopher, untarnished,
bearing the magic child across the stream.

Nancy Willard

For the Anniversary of My Death

Every year without knowing it I have passed the day
When the last fires will wave to me
And the silence will set out
Tireless traveller
Like the beam of a lightless star

Then I will no longer
Find myself in life as in a strange garment
Surprised at the earth
And the love of one woman
And the shamelessness of men
As today writing after three days of rain
Hearing the wren sing and the falling cease
And bowing not knowing to what

W. S. Merwin

Montauk Highway

Murderous middle age is my engine.

Harvey Shapiro

"Dr. Joel Hildebrand," *by Imogen Cunningham*

4

IN THE END WE
ARE ALL LIGHT

In The End We Are All Light

I love how old men carry purses for their wives,
those stiff light beige or navy wedge-shaped bags
that match the women's pumps,
with small gold clasps that click open and shut.
The men drowse off in medical center waiting rooms,
with bags perched in their laps like big tame birds
too worn to flap away. Within, the wives slowly undress,
put on the thin white robes, consult, come out
and wake the husbands dreaming openmouthed.

And when they both rise up
to take their constitutional,
walk up and down the block, her arms are free as air,
his right hand dangles down.

So I, desiring to shed this skin
for some light silken one,
will tell my husband, "Here, hold this,"
and watch him amble off into the mall among the shining
cans of motor oil, my leather bag
slung over his massive shoulder bone,
so prettily slender-waisted, so forgiving of the ways
we hold each other down, that watching him
I see how men love women, and women men,
and how the burden of the other comes to be
light as a feather blown, more quickly vanishing.

Liz Rosenberg

from The Rubáiyát

Tomorrow I will haul down the flag of hypocrisy,
I will devote my grey hairs to wine:
My life's span has reached seventy,
If I don't enjoy myself now, when shall I?

Omar Khayyám,
translation by Peter Avery and John Heath-Stubbs

The Superseded

I

As newer comers crowd the fore,
  We drop behind.
—We who have laboured long and sore
  Times out of mind,
And keen are yet, must not regret
  To drop behind.

II

Yet there are some of us who grieve
  To go behind;
Staunch, strenuous souls who scarce believe
  Their fires declined,
And know none spares, remembers, cares
  Who go behind.

III

'Tis not that we have unforetold
  The drop behind;
We feel the new must oust the old
  In every kind;
But yet we think, must we, must *we,*
  Too, drop behind?

Thomas Hardy

The Lamentation of the Old Pensioner

Although I shelter from the rain
Under a broken tree
My chair was nearest to the fire
In every company
That talked of love or politics,
Ere Time transfigured me.

Though lads are making pikes again
For some conspiracy,
And crazy rascals rage their fill
At human tyranny,
My contemplations are of Time
That has transfigured me.

There's not a woman turns her face
Upon a broken tree,
And yet the beauties that I loved
Are in my memory;
I spit into the face of Time
That has transfigured me.

William Butler Yeats

On Aging

When you see me sitting quietly,
Like a sack left on the shelf,
Don't think I need your chattering.
I'm listening to myself.
Hold! Stop! Don't pity me!
Hold! Stop your sympathy!
Understanding if you got it,
Otherwise I'll do without it!

When my bones are stiff and aching
And my feet won't climb the stair,
I will only ask one favor:
Don't bring me no rocking chair.

When you see me walking, stumbling,
Don't study and get it wrong.
'Cause tired don't mean lazy
And every goodbye ain't gone.
I'm the same person I was back then,
A little less hair, a little less chin,
A lot less lungs and much less wind.
But ain't I lucky I can still breathe in.

Maya Angelou

For the Record

in memory of Eleanor Bumpurs

Call out the colored girls
and the ones who call themselves Black
and the ones who hate the word nigger
and the ones who are very pale

Who will count the big fleshy women
the grandmother weighing 22 stone
with the rusty braids
and a gap-toothed scowl
who wasn't afraid of Armageddon
the first shotgun blast tore her right arm off
the one with the butcher knife
the second blew out her heart
through the back of her chest
and I am going to keep writing it down
how they carried her body out of the house
dress torn   up around her waist
uncovered
past tenants and the neighborhood children
a mountain of Black Woman
and I am going to keep telling this
if it kills me
and it might in ways I am
learning

The next day Indira Gandhi
was shot down in her garden
and I wonder what these two 67-year-old
colored girls
are saying to each other now
planning their return
and they weren't even
sisters.

Audre Lorde

An Old Woman

An old woman grabs
hold of your sleeve
and tags along.

She wants a fifty paise coin.
She says she will take you
to the horseshoe shrine.

You've seen it already.
She hobbles along anyway
and tightens her grip on your shirt.

She won't let you go.
You know how old women are.
They stick to you like a burr.

You turn around and face her
with an air of finality.
You want to end the farce.

When you hear her say,
"What else can an old woman do
on hills as wretched as these?"

You look right at the sky.
Clear through the bullet holes
she has for her eyes.

And as you look on,
the cracks that begin around her eyes
spread beyond her skin.

And the hills crack.
And the temples crack.
And the sky falls

with a plateglass clatter
around the shatter proof crone
who stands alone.

And you are reduced
to so much small change
in her hand.

Arun Kolatkar

To Waken an Old Lady

Old age is
a flight of small
cheeping birds
skimming
bare trees
above a snow glaze.
Gaining and failing
they are buffeted
by a dark wind—
But what?
On harsh weedstalks
the flock has rested,
the snow
is covered with broken
seedhusks
and the wind tempered
by a shrill
piping of plenty.

William Carlos Williams

"That time of year thou mayst in me behold" [73]

That time of year thou mayst in me behold
When yellow leaves, or none, or few, do hang
Upon those boughs which shake against the cold,
Bare ruined choirs where late the sweet birds sang.
In me thou seest the twilight of such day
As after sunset fadeth in the west,
Which by and by black night doth take away,
Death's second self, that seals up all in rest.
In me thou seest the glowing of such fire
That on the ashes of his youth doth lie,
As the deathbed whereon it must expire,
Consumed with that which it was nourished by.
   This thou perceiv'st, which makes thy love more
       strong,
   To love that well which thou must leave ere long.

William Shakespeare

Fable

Does everyone have to die? *Yes, everyone.*
Isn't there some way I can arrange
Not to die—cannot I take some strange
Prescription that my physician might know of?

No. I think not, not for money or love:
Everyone has to die, yes, everyone.

Cannot my banker and his bank provide,
Like a trust fund, for me to live on inside
My warm bright house and not be put into
A casket in the clay, can they not do
That for me and charge a fixed per cent
Like interest or taxes or the rent?

No, Madame, I fear not, and if they could
There might be more harm in it than good.

Merrill Moore

Arbor

As a child she planted
these roses, these vines
heavy with trumpets and honey.

Now at the end of her life
she asks for an arbor. At night
she sees roses rooted in heaven,

wisteria hanging its vineyards
over her head, all green things
climbing, climbing.

She wants to walk through this door,
not as she walks to the next
room but to another place

altogether. She will leave her cane
at the door but the door is
necessary. She knows how the raw

space in a wall nearly burned or
newly born makes children pause
and step in. It leads somewhere.

They look out on another country.

Nancy Willard

Eldorado

    Gaily bedight,
    A gallant knight,
In sunshine and in shadow,
    Had journeyed long,
    Singing a song,
In search of Eldorado.

    But he grew old—
    This knight so bold—
And o'er his heart a shadow
    Fell as he found
    No spot of ground
That looked like Eldorado.

    And, as his strength
    Failed him at length,
He met a pilgrim shadow—
    "Shadow," said he,
    "Where can it be—
This land of Eldorado?"

    "Over the Mountains
    Of the Moon,
Down the Valley of the Shadow,
    Ride, boldly ride,"
    The shade replied,—
"If you seek for Eldorado!"

Edgar Allan Poe

"I heard a Fly buzz–when I died"
[465]

I heard a Fly buzz—when I died—
The Stillness in the Room
Was like the Stillness in the Air—
Between the Heaves of Storm—

The Eyes around—had wrung them dry—
And Breaths were gathering firm
For that last Onset—when the King
Be witnessed—in the Room—

I willed my Keepsakes—Signed away
What portion of me be
Assignable—and then it was
There interposed a Fly—

With Blue—uncertain stumbling Buzz—
Between the light—and me—
And then the Windows failed—and then
I could not see to see—

Emily Dickinson

Fiddler Jones

The earth keeps some vibration going
There in your heart, and that is you.
And if the people find you can fiddle,
Why, fiddle you must, for all your life.
What do you see, a harvest of clover?
Or a meadow to walk through to the river?
The wind's in the corn; you rub your hands
For beeves hereafter ready for market;
Or else you hear the rustle of skirts
Like the girls when dancing at Little Grove.
To Cooney Potter a pillar of dust
Or whirling leaves meant ruinous drouth;
They looked to me like Red-Head Sammy
Stepping it off, to "Toor-a-Loor."
How could I till my forty acres
Not to speak of getting more,
With a medley of horns, bassoons and piccolos
Stirred in my brain by crows and robins
And the creak of a wind-mill—only these?
And I never started to plow in my life
That some one did not stop in the road
And take me away to a dance or picnic.
I ended up with forty acres;
I ended up with a broken fiddle—
And a broken laugh, and a thousand memories.
And not a single regret.

Edgar Lee Masters

Old Roger

Old Roger is dead and gone to his grave,
He, Hi, gone to his grave.
They planted an apple-tree over his head,
He, Hi, over his head.
The apples grew ripe and ready to drop,
He, Hi, ready to drop.
There came an old woman of Hipertihop,
He, Hi, Hipertihop,
She began a picking them up,
He, Hi, picking them up,
Old Roger got up and gave her a knock,
He, Hi, gave her a knock,
Which made the old woman go Hipertihop,
He, Hi, Hipertihop.

Anonymous

from Dead, adj.

Done with the work of breathing; done
With all the world; the mad race run
Through to the end; the golden goal
Attained—and found to be a hole!

Ambrose Bierce

My Own Epitaph

Life is a jest, and all things show it;
I thought so once, but now I know it.

John Gay

Epitaph

I never cared for Life: Life cared for me,
And hence I owed it some fidelity.
It now says, "Cease; at length thou hast learnt to grind
Sufficient toll for an unwilling mind,
And I dismiss thee—not without regard
That thou didst ask no ill-advised reward,
Nor sought in me much more than thou couldst find."

Thomas Hardy

"She drank good ale, strong punch and wine"

Epitaph to MRS FRELAND,
in Edwelton churchyard, Nottinghamshire, 1741

She drank good ale, strong punch and wine,
    And lived to the age of ninety-nine.

Anonymous

NOTES

The work of most of the poets anthologized in Lifelines *is available in volumes of collected or selected poems that you can find in your local library or bookstore.*

BELLA AKHMADULINA (b. 1937) was born in Moscow and came of age in Soviet Russia, during the relatively liberal-minded early 1960s, when the public's enthusiasm for poetry was such that important readings drew capacity crowds in a Moscow sports stadium. Akhmadulina was married for a time to Russia's most famous poet, Yevgeny Yevtushenko; though her name is less well known internationally than his, readers of Russian poetry admire Akhmadulina's piquant writings equally and in some cases more.

YEHUDA AMICHAI (b. 1924), who was born in Würzburg, Germany, and emigrated to Palestine in 1936, is Israel's leading poet. The special power of his poetry stems from his ability to link his personal experience, about which he writes with passion and verve, to the ancient stories and imagery of the Jewish people.

MAYA ANGELOU (b. 1928) has worked as a singer, editor, actress, television screenwriter, composer, and educator. She is the author of such autobiographical works as *I Know Why the Caged Bird Sings* (1970) and *All God's Children Need Traveling Shoes* (1986), and several volumes of verse. In January 1993, millions of people worldwide heard Angelou read her poem "On the Pulse of Morning" at the inauguration of President Bill Clinton.

W. H. AUDEN (1907–1973) was born in York, England, and later came to live in the United States, eventually becoming a U.S. citizen. One of the most influential writers of his generation, Auden was a public poet who forcefully commented in his poetry on the great issues of his time, including the morality of war and the nature of modern mass culture.

MARIA BANUS (b. 1914) is one of Romania's most respected writers. She has published poetry, plays, and translations from five languages, including works by the German poet Rainer Maria Rilke, the French poet Arthur Rimbaud, and the Chilean poet Pablo Neruda.

FRANCES BAZIL (b. 1948) is a Coeur d'Alene Indian. She has studied writing at the Institute of American Indian Arts in Santa Fe, New Mexico. In 1965 "Uncertain Admission" won first prize in poetry in the under-sixteen category at the Scottsdale (Arizona) National Indian Arts Exhibition.

AMBROSE BIERCE (1842–1914?) was a San Francisco journalist and pundit known for his bleak, razor-sharp wit and generally dim view of humanity. In late 1913 he left for Mexico under mysterious circumstances and was not heard from again.

ELIZABETH BISHOP (1911–1979) A master storyteller and master of poetic forms, Bishop, who was born in Worcester, Massachusetts, lived much of her adult life in Brazil. The dry wit and offhand manner of her poems have the quality of supremely good conversation. To achieve this appearance of effort-lessness, however, Bishop, in draft after patient draft, weighed each of her words with exacting care.

WILLIAM BLAKE (1757–1827), who was dismissed by many during his lifetime as a madman, has since been recognized as one of England's most original creative artists. Blake illustrated, as well as printed, much of his own verse, interweaving image and text to produce a fascinating new art form—a forerunner to the modern picture book. This poet observed: "The road of excess leads to the palace of wisdom"; and "No bird soars too high, if he soars with his own wings."

GWENDOLYN BROOKS (b. 1917) began writing poetry at the age of seven and has been a civil rights activist since the 1940s. Of the young pool players of "We Real Cool" Brooks has remarked: "These are people who are essentially saying, 'Kilroy is here. We *are*.' But they're a little uncertain of the strength of their identity. . . . I want[ed] to represent their basic uncertainty."

ELEANOR CAMERON (b. 1912), who was born in Canada and now lives in California, is the author of novels, essays, and award-winning children's books, including the well-loved *The Wonderful Flight to the Mushroom Planet* (1954), which she wrote at the request of her then seven-year-old son David. This poem about her son is the second she has published.

ROBERT CREELEY (b. 1926), who was a member of the remarkable group of experimental writers and artists who taught during the 1950s at North Carolina's Black Mountain College, is a poetic minimalist. His fastidiously crafted verses have a haunting, tip-of-the-iceberg quality about them, leaving the uncanny impression that the poem on the page is only a fragment (though a *telling* frag-ment) of something still to be said.

EMILY DICKINSON (1830–1886) was born in Amherst, Massachusetts, the daughter of a respected lawyer, and lived in the same Amherst house nearly all her life. She published only seven of her more than seventeen hundred poems during her lifetime—all anonymously. Dickinson wrote poems of bracing clarity that have the urgency and compressed drama of telegrams. She offered a friend this self-portrait: "I . . . am small, like the wren; and my hair is bold, like the chestnut burr; and my eyes, like the sherry in the glass that the guest leaves."

RAY DUREM (1915–1963) is represented in *The Black Poets* (1971), edited by Dudley Randall. Here he makes a powerful poetic—and political—statement by angrily rejecting traditional notions about what poetry can and should be like.

RICHARD EDWARDS (b. 1949) is a poet who has made a specialty of writing witty, insightful, sympathetic rhymes about the experience of being very young. Among his recent books is *The Word Party* (1992).

EDWARD FIELD (b. 1924) was born in Brooklyn, New York. Fellow poet Stanley Moss has written that Field's poems are "almost stories—open, readable, available. His honesty is close to beauty. His best poems . . . tell beautiful and believable stories of the indestructibility of the human spirit, at a time when most human energies and resources are perversely wasted or destroyed."

KATHLEEN FRASER (b. 1937) was born in Tulsa, Oklahoma, and now lives in San Francisco. Concerning her reasons for writing, she has said: "Sometimes it is specific things that need out, need expression. Other times it is simply a pure joy sensation that wants celebration. And sometimes it is simply the need to write, not knowing what."

JOHN GAY (1685–1732), an English poet and playwright, was a friend of two of eighteenth-century England's literary lions, the satirists Alexander Pope and Jonathan Swift, whose careers nearly always overshadowed his own. Gay's moment came with the spectacular success on the London stage of his *The Beggar's Opera* (1728), a dramatic comedy that slyly comments on the similarities between gentlemen and thieves.

MEL GLENN (b. 1943) was born in Switzerland, grew up in Brooklyn, New York, and served as a Peace Corps volunteer in West Africa during the 1960s. He now teaches English at the Brooklyn high school that he once attended as a student. He is the author of several volumes of poems about high school life, including *Class Dismissed!* (1982) and *My Friend's Got This Problem, Mr. Candler* (1991).

THOMAS HARDY (1840–1928) was one of the few writers to create major works of both fiction and poetry. His novels, all of which are set in the region of southern England where he was born, include *The Return of the Native* (1878), *The Mayor of Casterbridge* (1886), and *Jude the Obscure* (1896).

GERARD MANLEY HOPKINS (1844–1889) was an English Jesuit priest who produced a small body of wondrously original verse. The strange music of Hopkins's poetry is what readers usually first notice about it. Then, as the poems become more familiar, they "explode" with meaning, as Hopkins himself said. In "Spring and Fall" the poet has used accent marks to show which syllables should receive special stress when reading the poem aloud.

DAVID IGNATOW (b. 1914), who was born in Brooklyn, New York, writes in a deliberately matter-of-fact voice in poems that might be the news dispatches of an unusually knowing and brutally honest reporter.

SAMUEL JOHNSON (1709–1784) was one of eighteenth-century England's most brilliant and versatile writers. Along with a hefty volume's worth of verse, Johnson authored numerous essays, biographies, travelogues, satires, and reviews, and the English language's first dictionary. "To a poet," Johnson once said, "nothing can be useless."

DONALD JUSTICE (b. 1925) is an American poet whose work is a cunning fusion of stark understatement and extravagant perception. He taught for many years at the University of Iowa's pioneering Writers Workshop and currently teaches at the University of Florida at Gainesville.

GALWAY KINNELL (b. 1927) emerged during the 1960s as a leading figure within the astonishing generation of American poets that also includes W. S. Merwin, James Wright, Mark Strand, Donald Justice, and several others represented here. His lyrical poems are filled with a sense of life's sadness, outlandishness, and beauty.

RUDYARD KIPLING (1865–1936) was born of English parents in British colonial India, a world about which he later wrote. While still in his twenties, Kipling achieved considerable fame as both a poet and short-story writer. He went on to produce many books for children and adults, including the fables of *The Jungle Books* (1894 and 1895) and *Just So Stories* (1902); the stories about school life of *Stalky & Co.* (1899); and the novel *Kim* (1901).

ARUN KOLATKAR (b. 1932) is a poet of India who writes in both Marathi and English, the first language of 1 to 2 percent of India's 850 million inhabitants. His first English-language poetry collection is *Jejuri* (1976). He works as a graphic artist in Bombay.

FREDA LAUGHTON (b. 1907) This little-known Irish poet is represented in Kathleen Hoagland's landmark anthology, *1000 Years of Irish Poetry* (1947). Laughton also wrote and illustrated fairy tales.

JOHN LOGAN (1923–1987) described poetry as "a ballet for the ear." *"Saltimbanque"* is a French word for "tumbler" and "juggler"; as the two brothers of Logan's poem struggle to keep their balance—and dignity—while standing at the end of a moving train, the rhythm of the poem *becomes* the train's motion for readers.

AUDRE LORDE (1934–1993) refused, according to fellow poet Adrienne Rich, to be "circumscribed by any simple identity." She wrote "as a Black woman, a mother, a daughter, a Lesbian, a feminist, a visionary." "For the Record" concerns actual events that took place in October 1984: In New York City, Eleanor Bumpurs was killed by police who were attempting to evict her from her city-owned apartment. In India, Prime Minister Indira Gandhi was assassinated at her home near New Delhi.

EDGAR LEE MASTERS (1869–1950) was born in Kansas and practiced law in Chicago for thirty years while also building a reputation as a writer. Fiddler Jones is one of 244 characters who speak their own epitaphs from the grave in Masters's best-known work, *Spoon River Anthology* (1915), which can be read as a pithy chronicle of small-town American life around the turn of the century or as a wide-ranging survey of human folly and fate.

HERMAN MELVILLE (1819–1891) is primarily known today for his epic novel *Moby-Dick* (1851), but during his lifetime it was for earlier writings like *Typee* (1846), which chronicled his own far-flung adventures at sea, that Melville won a measure of renown. In mid-career, he turned to the shorter literary form of lyric poetry. In his first verse collection, *Battle-Pieces* (1866), Melville set down his impressions of the just-concluded American Civil War.

W. S. MERWIN (b. 1927), who was Galway Kinnell's classmate at Princeton, electrified readers in the 1960s and '70s with his spare but metaphorically striking free verse. Merwin, who now lives in Hawaii, has also translated the work of the Russian poet Osip Mandelstam, the French poet Jean Follain, and others.

JOSEPHINE MILES (1911–1985) was born in Chicago and for many years taught literature at the University of California at Berkeley. Like Emily Dickinson, she wrote with such clarity and precision that her poems have the power to make old, familiar words feel freshly minted.

WILLIAM COSMO MONKHOUSE (1840–1901) was a Victorian poet and scholar who wrote several books about the British artists of his day, as well as two volumes of verse, *Corn and Poppies* (1890) and *Lyrics* (1900).

MERRILL MOORE (1903–1957) was a psychiatrist with a remarkable knack for sonnet writing. Moore composed hundreds of the fourteen-line rhymed poems. Such was his proficiency at the genre that it is said he could polish off a complete sonnet while waiting for the light to change at the wheel of his car.

OGDEN NASH (1902–1971) dropped out of Harvard, had a brief, lackluster career on Wall Street, worked on the staff of *The New Yorker* for all of three months, and then found his calling as a writer of shrewd, deliciously playful comic verse. Nash published his poems in *Esquire, Good Housekeeping, The New Yorker*, and many other magazines, and in a succession of popular books.

FRANK O'HARA (1926–1966) worked as an art critic and associate curator at the Museum of Modern Art in New York while writing the exuberant, bad-boyish poetry for which he became well known before his untimely, accidental death. His lively essays on such American artists as Jackson Pollock and Franz Kline are gathered in *Art Chronicles* (1975). His pocket-size verse collection, *Lunch Poems* (1964), is a treat.

OMAR KHAYYÁM (1048?–1123?) was a Persian poet and intellectual who first made a name for himself as a mathematician and astronomer. He was also widely known in his lifetime as a philosopher, historian, and legal and medical scholar. "Rubáiyát" is a Persian word meaning "quatrain," or four-line rhymed verse. The unbridled sensuality of Omar's collection of such verses caused a great stir in the West with the publication of Edward FitzGerald's first English-language translation in 1859.

AMBROSE PHILIPS (1675?–1749) was a satirical poet and a member of the circle of wits who gathered around the London essayist Joseph Addison. He held a variety of government posts, serving as a justice of the peace, a commissioner of the lottery, a judge, and a member of the Irish Parliament.

EDGAR ALLAN POE (1809–1849) was a literary rebel who wrote dark, mysterious, passionate poems and stories at a time when many American readers expected their literature to be morally uplifting and properly genteel. Unappreciated during his lifetime, Poe is today remembered as the author of some of the most broodingly evocative poetry in English and as an early master both of the horror story and of detective fiction.

KATHA POLLITT (b. 1949) was born in New York City. Her critically acclaimed first book of poems is *Antarctic Traveller* (1982). She is associate editor of *The Nation*.

RIHAKU (701–762), also known as Li Po, was a celebrated court poet who lived during the early period of China's Tang dynasty, a golden time in the arts that has been compared to England's Elizabethan age. Such was the esteem in which this lyric poet was held that he could openly satirize the emperor himself without fear of reprisal. His American translator, Ezra Pound (1885–1972), was one of the twentieth century's most influential and idiosyncratic experimental poets.

JAMES WHITCOMB RILEY (1849–1916) Known as "the Hoosier poet" and as "the most beloved citizen of Indiana," Riley drew large, enthusiastic crowds whenever he took to the lecture circuit to read his good-natured, folksy verses, many of which were written in the dialect of an uneducated Midwesterner of his day.

THEODORE ROETHKE (1908–1963) was born in Saginaw, Michigan, the son of a florist. His own close knowledge of plants and flowers became a rich source of inspiration for his poetic response to human experience. About his standard for poetry, Roethke remarked: "To produce the truly singable thing, that's a glory, isn't it?"

LIZ ROSENBERG (b. 1955) is a poet, critic, and author of children's books. Her most recent poetry collection is *Children of Paradise* (1993). Here she shows that she is a perceptive, full-hearted poet of the everyday.

NORMAN ROSTEN (b. 1914) is the poet laureate of Brooklyn, New York. He wrote *Songs for Patricia* (1951) for his daughter, who is now an artist. Among his works of fiction are *Under the Boardwalk* (1968) and *Neighborhood Tales* (1986).

WILLIAM SHAKESPEARE (1564–1616) is English literature's preeminent poet and playwright. Almost four hundred years after his death, Shakespeare's plays are in constant production throughout the world. Recently two of them, *Henry V* and *Much Ado About Nothing*, were made into feature-length films by actor-director Kenneth Branagh. Shakespeare, who seems never to have lacked for words on any subject, composed this epitaph for himself:

> Good friend, for Jesus' sake forbear
> To dig the dust enclosed here;
> Blest be the man that spares these stones,
> And curst be he that moves my bones.

HARVEY SHAPIRO (b. 1924) was born in Chicago and has for many years been an editor at *The New York Times*. His books of poetry include *Lauds* (1975) and *National Cold Storage Company* (1988).

STEVIE SMITH (1902–1971) lived in London, where she wrote three novels and a substantial sheaf of witty, often caustic rhymed poetry. In poems that have the singsong rhythm of nursery nonsense, Smith led readers past innocence to her own acutely drawn, quirky view of the human condition. Her life is the subject of the film *Stevie* (1978).

WILLIAM STAFFORD (1914–1993) was born in Kansas and later lived and taught in Oregon. A genial, open-faced man and a prolific writer, Stafford often dazzled audiences by reading a poem he had composed earlier the same day. His ability to write regularly reflected his poetic, and spiritual, creed: that people encountered, moments glimpsed, and conversations recalled all hold significance worthy of a poet's best language. One of his three children was a daughter named Kit.

ROBERT LOUIS STEVENSON (1850–1894), whom friends called Louis, was born in Edinburgh, Scotland, to a noted family of lighthouse engineers. A sickly child, he took to novel writing while still a teenager. During a brief, comet-like career that was marked equally by high adventure and ill health, Stevenson produced numerous and varied writings, including the adventure stories *Treasure Island* (1883) and *Kidnapped* (1886); *A Child's Garden of Verses* (1885); and the psychological horror story *The Strange Case of Dr. Jekyll and Mr. Hyde* (1886).

MARK STRAND (b. 1934), who was born on Prince Edward Island, Canada, was a painter before he became a poet. Visually arresting, surreal images are among the memorable features of his poetry. In 1990 Strand was chosen by the Librarian of Congress to be poet laureate of the United States. He currently teaches at the University of Utah in Salt Lake City.

E. B. WHITE (1899–1985), who was born in Mount Vernon, New York, first made his reputation as one of *The New Yorker*'s wittiest staff writers. During a long and varied career, he authored personal essays, journalism, light verse, three children's books, including the immortal *Charlotte's Web* (1952), and co-authored with his old teacher William Strunk Jr. *The Elements of Style* (1959), a down-to-earth and delightful handbook for writers.

NANCY WILLARD (b. 1936) teaches English at Vassar College. She is a poet, novelist, short story writer, and author of children's books, including *A Visit to William Blake's Inn* (1981). A fantasist, Willard takes equal pleasure in the beauty and the strangeness of life—and words. She has commented: "Each work chooses its own form. . . . They all come from the same well."

WILLIAM CARLOS WILLIAMS (1883–1963) was a medical doctor and an experimental poet who brought a new lustiness and sensuality to American poetry. A skilled practitioner of free verse, he declared that a poem is "a machine made of words" in which "there can be no part . . . that is redundant."

WILLIAM WORDSWORTH (1770–1850) was one of the central figures of the English Romantic movement of poets and writers. He believed that children have an inborn spiritual sense and an appreciation of nature that are usually lost by the time adulthood is attained. To Wordsworth, lucky is the grown man or woman with an authentically childlike view of reality.

JAMES WRIGHT (1927–1980) was born in the industrial town of Martins Ferry, Ohio, a grim place that provided the subject and setting of many of his plain-spoken, deeply compassionate poems. Among the characters who inhabit Wright's mournful but celebratory lyrics are factory workers, high school full-backs, town drunks, and Ohio-born president Warren G. Harding.

ELINOR WYLIE (1885–1928) was born into an old New England family and raised in opulent circumstances in Washington, D.C. During a brief, tumultuous life, Wylie married three times and published four volumes of poetry and as many novels.

WILLIAM BUTLER YEATS (1865–1939) was Ireland's greatest poet. As a young man Yeats developed a passion for Irish mythology and incorporated themes and characters from the ancient lore in his poetry. In his later years, he proceeded to devise a mythology of his own, writing in a more "personal" voice that is nonetheless richly laden with heroic and tragic overtones. Yeats was a cofounder of the Irish National Theatre. His *Autobiographies* (1926) is a spirited tale well told.

■

The work of the following photographers appears in Lifelines.

LEON A. BORENSZTEIN (b. 1947) was born in Poland and educated in Israel and at the San Francisco Art Institute. Concern for the mistreatment of animals was a passionate theme of this accomplished photographer's early work. More recently, Borensztein has concentrated on portraiture, photographing his family, athletes from the Special Olympics, and others. He lives in Oakland, California.

IMOGEN CUNNINGHAM (1883–1976) An American master long associated with the San Francisco Bay Area, Cunningham remained at photography's cutting edge for a remarkable seventy years. The artist was in her early nineties when she created *After Ninety*, published a year after her death, a book of portraits of fellow nonagenarians, from which the photograph reproduced here was chosen.

BRUCE DAVIDSON (b. 1933) has been a professional photographer since 1946. The double portrait reprinted in *Lifelines* is from his *East 100th Street* series, a photo-essay published in book form and exhibited at the Museum of Modern Art, New York, in 1970. Davidson's photographs have been the subject of numerous other books and exhibitions.

ABELARDO MORELL (b. 1948) The work of this innovative Cuban-born photographer is included in the permanent collections of the Museum of Modern Art, New York; the Metropolitan Museum of Art; the San Francisco Museum of Modern Art; and other major institutions. The recipient of a 1993–94 Guggenheim Fellowship, Morell has exhibited widely. He lives in Brookline, Massachusetts.

NICHOLAS NIXON (b. 1947) Nixon's emotionally riveting black-and-white photographs were the subject of the exhibition Pictures of People (and of a book of the same name), which originated at New York's Museum of Modern Art in 1988 and toured nationally. Each year since 1975, Nixon has produced a group portrait of his wife Bebe and her three sisters. The photograph shown in *Lifelines* belongs to this Brown Sisters series; the photographer's wife is second from the right.

JIM VARRIALE (b. 1953) began his career in 1978 working for photographer Richard Avedon. Since then he has become known in his own right as a photographer specializing in portraiture, fashion, and commercial photography. His work has appeared in *Vogue*, *Mirabella*, *Rolling Stone*, *Life*, and other magazines. Dance is a personal enthusiasm of Varriale's: his frontispiece photograph is one of a series taken at The New Ballet School, in New York City.

ACKNOWLEDGMENTS

Every effort has been made to trace the copyright holders of the material included in this anthology. The publisher regrets any possible omissions and would be glad to hear from any current copyright holder whose name does not appear below.

POEMS

"To a New-Born Child," by William Cosmo Monkhouse. From Corn and Poppies *by William Cosmo Monkhouse.* ■ *"Infant Joy,"* by William Blake. From Selected Poetry and Prose of William Blake, *edited by Northrop Frye.* ■ *"To Miss Charlotte Pulteney in Her Mother's Arms,"* by Ambrose Philips. From The New Oxford Book of Eighteenth Century Verse, *edited by Roger Lonsdale.* ■ *"Conch,"* by E. B. White. From Poems and Sketches of E. B. White. *Copyright © 1948 by E. B. White. Reprinted by permission of HarperCollins Publishers.* ■ *"To David—At Six Months,"* by Eleanor Cameron. *Copyright © 1994 by Eleanor Cameron. Used by permission of the author.* ■ *"This is my name,"* by Norman Rosten. From Songs for Patricia *by Norman Rosten. Copyright © 1951, 1979, 1988 by Norman Rosten. Reprinted by permission of Harold Ober Associates Incorporated.* ■ *"Mutterings Over the Crib of a Deaf Child,"* by James Wright. From Collected Poems *by James Wright. Copyright © 1957 by James Wright. Wesleyan University Press by permission of University Press of New England.* ■ *"Baby, baby,"* Anonymous. ■ *"When I Was Three,"* by Richard Edwards. From The Word Party *by Richard Edwards. Text copyright © 1986 and 1987 by Richard Edwards. Reprinted by permission of Lutterworth Press.* ■ *"Human Affection,"* by Stevie Smith. From The Collected Poems of Stevie Smith *by Stevie Smith. Copyright © 1973 by Stevie Smith. Reprinted by permission of New Directions Publishing Corporation.* ■ *"The Hired Man's Faith in Children,"* by James Whitcomb Riley. From The Best of James Whitcomb Riley, *edited by Donald C. Manlove.* ■ *"God made the bees,"* Anonymous. From The Lore and Language of Schoolchildren *by Iona and Peter Opie, 1959. Reprinted by permission of Oxford University Press.* ■ *"The Swing,"* by Robert Louis Stevenson. From A Child's Garden of Verses *by Robert Louis Stevenson.* ■ *"A Poem by Garnie Braxton,"* by James Wright. From Collected Poems *by James Wright. Copyright © 1971 by James Wright. Wesleyan University Press by permission of University Press of New England.* ■ *"In the Waiting Room,"* by Elizabeth Bishop. From The Complete Poems 1927–1979 *by Elizabeth Bishop. Copyright © 1979, 1983 by Alice Helen Methfessel. Reprinted by permission of Farrar, Straus and Giroux, Inc.* ■ *"Ethiopia,"* by Audre Lorde. *Reprinted from* Our Dead Behind Us, Poems by Audre Lorde, *by permission of W. W. Norton & Company, Inc. Copyright © 1986 by Audre Lorde.* ■ *"First Song,"* by Galway Kinnell. From What a Kingdom It Was *by Galway Kinnell. Copyright © 1960, © renewed 1988 by Galway Kinnell. Reprinted by permission of Houghton Mifflin Company. All rights reserved.* ■ *"Spring and Fall,"* by Gerard Manley Hopkins. From Gerard Manley Hopkins: Poems and Prose, *edited by W. H. Gardner.* ■ *"The Conventionalist,"* by Stevie Smith. From The Collected Poems of Stevie Smith *by Stevie Smith. Copyright © 1972 by Stevie Smith. Reprinted by permission of New Directions Publishing Corporation.* ■ *"The Brothers: Two Saltimbanques,"* by John Logan. *Copyright © 1989 by the John Logan Literary Estate, Inc. Reprinted from* John Logan: The Collected Poems *with the permission of BOA Editions, Ltd., 92 Park Avenue, Brockport, New York 14420.* ■ *"Dresses,"* by Kathleen Fraser. From In Defiance *by Kathleen Fraser. Copyright © 1969 by Kathleen Fraser.*

INDEX